Alex Gordon Alexander Biography

Alex joined the Royal Signals on 1st Septem... tice college (Harrogate) once he had completed hi... Germany, deploying on his first operational ...rning to Germany he completed a course and served ...rs later he was posted back to the UK and serv... Op Warden (Turkey) following his return was in... a unit move to Nuneaton, once in Nuneaton he deployed on Operations in Bosnia (Former Republic of Yugoslavia) Op Grapple and Op Chantress (Angola) following his posting to Nuneaton he was sent to Catterick where he carried out further deployments to Bosnia and Kosovo. He was then posted as a Corporal to Herford, Germany. Where he served in Oman, and was promoted to Sergeant. He then returned to Blandford as a Trade Instructor for phase 2 and Phase 3 trainees. After 18months in Blandford he was again posted to 7th Armoured Brigade in Germany doing exercises in Poland, and deploying on Operation Telic in Iraq, he was then posted again within Germany to carry out 2 tours of Afghanistan where he was selected for promotion to Staff Sergeant. After serving in 7th Signal Regiment he was then posted back to the UK for his final posting to 3 (UK) Division and Signal Regiment. Deploying on another tour of Afghanistan serving in Mob Price with the Danish Battle Group followed by 2 Parachute Regiment.
On his return he worked in the training wing after all his military service earning a deserved rest however this changed when he had to become a Troop SSgt once again.

Alex was a avid rugby player in both Rugby Union and Rugby League, He was a qualified Coach and Referee his highlight being refereeing The British Army Germany against Australia where he earned man of the match.

Since leaving the military he has raised over £2500 for charities such as Combat Stress and Veterans United against Suicide. Which he is passionate about due to suffering with CPTSD himself. He has lost many friends through suicide and mental health issues. This book denotes some of the poetry he has written as eulogies for those lost friends and also some of his darker times during his struggle with his mental health. He has also managed to help others with some of his poetry as it gives people the strength to realize that they are not alone and he is an advocate for Military groups being setup where all services can enjoy likeminded banter together in a safe place.

WHY I WRITE POETRY

Poetry is putting emotions down in verse
Good for those that cannot converse
I don't think I'm very good
But it keeps me out of the lonely wood

The lonely wood is a very sad place
The gremlins and ghouls change your face
It's dark and dank very austere
Poetry is my voice I hope you hear

I write my poems they lead me away
From the woods it's a bad place to play
The dark and smell gets into your mind
You can't see your going blind

Writing lets me see the light
Helps me to feel alright
I know it's only a small fix
Better than surrounded by sticks

So when I hurt or don't understand
A pen and paper comes to hand
It helps me see what I need to do
Pulls me out of feeling so blue

It may not work for everyone
Some listen to their favourite song
But this poetry thing for me
Clears all of my anxiety

Yes some may say it's in the mind
Solutions to help are hard to find
This is the one that I find best
Gets all the hurt off my chest

So when you don't know where to turn
Keep out of them woods or you will burn
Find your release in your safe place
Help you put the smile on your face

Believe in your own self is a must
Otherwise you'll end up like dust
No one deserves to feel like that
Conquer those demons bury that hat

Feel free to say whatever is on the mind
To yourself try to be kind
Don't let it beat you up anymore
It's your _LIFE_ not a chore

I hope this helps someone out there
Because people are people some do care
If it has feel free to say
let other know what's your way

BASIC TRAINING DAY 1

For it was 29 years ago
When as I boy I left home
On the train other lads I find
Apprehensive blind leading the blind

When we got to our destination
Shouting started is this an hallucination
Standing still waiting for orders
That corporal from the Scottish Borders

Get on the bus he shouts at us
Some of the lads begin to cus
The transport takes us through the gates
Some may say this place I hate

Marched around real fast
Shown our accommodation at last
Sitting waiting for other lads to show
Some just say I got to go

The peace is broken with a shout
Everyone get out, get out
We all mingle on that damp night
Sergeant shouting gives us a fright

Welcome speech the stage was his
Ok boys haircuts it is
Prepare to double to the barbers shop
Hair on the floor could make a mop

After this was uniform time
Hurry up get in line
In this queue we had to wait
Issued clothes and a metal plate

Back to the room with all this kit
Placed into the locker by my pit
Then lights out at 10 pm
Wait for tomorrow's mayhem

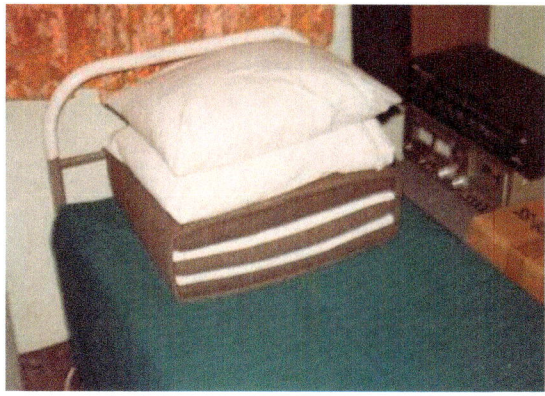

30 YEAR ANNIVERSARY

Thirty years since we signed on that line
The oath of allegiance to serve our time
We served our country and our queen
Far off lands and conflicts we have seen

87c was our intake
Many friends for life we did make
Just boys broken down again and again
Stuck together it made us men

Taught to march and iron all our kit
Lots of physical training to get us fit
Twelve man rooms along the corridor
See your face in the bumpered floor

Team work and a real passion
Got us through hard times to a fashion
Quick change parades and bull nights thrown in
The permanent staff thought they would win

Then after 12 weeks of basic training
Exercises come even when it was raining
Young warriors and external leadership
Plenty of shooting but not from the hip

Amongst all this stuff we learnt a trade
Only 16 but still getting paid
They tried to break us but they couldn't see

We were the mighty 87C

ARMISTACE DAY 2023

Eleventh of November is armistice day
A day in the year where we remember
Remember what I hear you say
The sacrifice of many far far away

They fought for freedom
Did not die in vain
Our lives would have changed
Those survivors still suffer the pain

The symbol is iconic
A red poppy is worn
This is a real topic
To remember those whose lives were torn

A sailor a soldier an airman involved
Whether supporting or on the front line
Their stories must remain being told
They all signed up and hoped to be fine

Casualties fall in conflict
This is a fact of war
Surviving there is no trick
Heads up and do your tour

So when you see them marching through your town
With shiny boots and medals on their chest
Give them respect and don't be a clown
These women and men have fought their best

Remember there not doing it for glory
It's for friends from conflicts they have lost
If you ask them of their story
Don't be offended if they don't host

Some may discuss their times away
Others may just clam up
Rest assured they remember everyday
If they do, please don't interrupt

This year remembrance falls on the twelfth
So when they are out and about
Salute and pray for good health
You may hear the Parade Marshall shout
British Legion FALL OUT

CRISIS SUPPORTERS

Comes many a different way
Raised heartbeat so they say
Insular in thought and deed
Support from others they do need

Intelligent listening and a free shoulder
Soldiers talk better to a soldiers
Stay with then until they are safe
Unifying brotherhood defying the strafe

Providing comfort and lending an ear
Prepared to even shed a tear
Order a coffee and have a chat
Remain positive be a diplomat

Try to stay focused on saving your buddy
Energy zapped thoughts going through your body
Remain calm positive and you will succeed
Stress is an injury that can't be seen

SLEEP TIGHT

Dreams and nightmares come and go
I've found something you ought to know
These night terrors can cause distress
Reading below could rid this mess

If you wake due to thrashing around
Tiredness and lethargy will be found
You can control your mind in sleep
Don't worry now , this isn't too deep

Management of subconscious mind
The answer to this I hope you find
Dreams are like a washing machine
When it's working , life is serene

When the machine breaks and overspills
Nightmares play and mayhem shrills
We need to fix this and stop it fast
Or decent sleep is a thing of the past

Common in trauma nightmares are
Distressing thoughts from lands afar
You're not alone this is for sure
Hopefully I can give you the cure

Don't try to analyse what's making you wake
It's only a nightmare for goodness sake
Too you I know its causes alarm
I'm just saying, it can't cause you any harm

It doesn't have to be logical or real
Along as you sleep that's the appeal
Keep this ending on an imaginary shelf
As you sleep it will assist in your health

When you wake If you can remember it
Think of an ending that will benefit
The ending can be anything you like
The nightmare will get on its bike

If this ending does not work
Whatever you do, don't go berserk
Try it again on the next night
Eventually you'll sleep without fright

If you don't remember when you wake
All is not lost use your feelings intake
You wake with fear and sweating hard
Change ending to a picturesque postcard

Keep practicing this changing technique
Then the nightmares will become weak
Persevere and see the light
All I can now, say is "SLEEP TIGHT,   GOODNIGHT"

FIREWORKS

It's new year's eve or bonfire night.
Veterans hide away in fright
They fear that they may crumble
As the fireworks start to rumble

Even if there tucked up in bed
The flashes and bangs mess up the head
Hot sweats, and uncontrollable shaking
It isn't fun that it's making

Some just say your a party pooper
Join us when were in our stupor
The nightmares start, flashbacks come
Yet again everyone have your fun

These actions cause much distress
Some more than others I confess
The symptoms mentioned before
Cannot hurt them that's for sure

But in their head It's like being back
On the edge under attack
Rounds and rockets whizzing by
That is why they break down and cry

Organised events aren't so bad
As that's a choice that can be had
Its the ones that go off Willy nilly
There the ones that make us silly

Spare a thought at this time of year
Bang less fireworks won't cause fear
So use these types if you can
Think about that veteran

It's not just them this affects
It even frightens house hold pets
I'm not trying to stop your fun
But think about others it needs to be done

YOU ARE NOT ALONE

You are not alone
Only you will disagree
Until you shout out and say
Alas no one else will see

Remember your friends and family are there
Everybody who knows you really do care
Now everybody can find this lonely place
Others manage to pull them out

There is light at the end of the tunnel
All people who experience this it's said
Loneliness is only in the head
Oh my that is not so

No one should ever feel alone
Everybody has people who care

Social media, telephone, just shout it is there

ARMISTACE DAY ACCROUSTIC

Armed with weapons to kill the enemy
Remember those who have died for your country
Many thousands throughout all the years
Individuals who survived still shedding tears
Stood on foreign soil fighting hard
Taking hits like a ball in the yard
Anywhere in the world our military deployed
Creating freedom, dictatorship we did avoid
Enemies come in all types of form
Dictators, terrorists world peace not the norm
All young men and women sign on the line
Your lives you'll give when it is time.

BLACK DOG CATCHER

What is the purpose of life?
Can't even keep your wife!
Then there's holding down a job.
Are you really that much of a snob.

Life is surely about family
Why can't it be for me
Am I that screwed up?
Over floweth does the cup

Is this just another blip
Or am I travelling on the one way ship
What is wrong with me
My loved ones I just cannot see

Why do I make them suffer
It's my fault I'm a bit rougher
They deserve better than me
They should have stability

Why do I feel alone
Can't even grab the phone
If only I was passed
The family would have tranquillity at last.

The black dog is on my shoulder
Really getting bolder and bolder
He can wait until I'm in focus
Then I can give him some hocus copus

Failing is something I can't do
Unfortunately this is not true
I am a massive failure
Larger than a 10 tonne trailer

I don't feel to good today
MENTAL HEALTH what can I say
Slashes on my arm to feel pain
What can I say about my brain

It hurts when you lose control
If I didn't the family would be whole
Not very nice when your thoughts are strong
When you feel you don't belong

Woke up today feeling embarrassed
Because of actions arms are a mess
But today will begin a new chapter
After all I am the Black Dog Catcher

SAFE PLACE

I sit on the cliff top
Watching the world go by
Listening to seagulls
Squawking in the sky

hearing waves crashing into the rocks
Wearing flip-flops without socks
Feeling the sun beating down on me
Oh how nice it is to be by the sea

This is my safe place
Out of the rat race
People walk past but Do not see
This ex-soldier taking in the scenery

The breeze passing past my face
I love it here in my safe place
Nothing can stop the feeling of content
I'm even thinking about pitching a tent

This way I could live without any stress
As sometime you feel your life's a mess
Find your safe place close to the sea
I promise you'll be content like me.

SUN SHINING HAIKU

The sun is shining

Time to do walking outside

Its good for the mind

ITS ABOUT PAIN HAIKU

All about the pain

Manifesting in your brain

It will disappear

MICKY ELLIOT RIP

It's so sad to hear the news today
Another brother has passed away
Mick Elliott is his name
This is Truly a real shame

Elly dog as he was known
A great bloke and mentor for all below
He didn't mince his words this is true
But always willing to help if you were in a stew

I first met mick in a place called Bramcote
Where people ran around without a coat
By coat I mean without a stitch
This was just some of the antics

501 jasper was his det
All his crew will never forget
I never served with him on tour
From what I hear it was never a chore

An FC Barnet fan he certainly was
Even if never winning was a cause
Always believing they'd win the FA Cup
Oh micky boy never happen so shut up!

Never offended or hurt by his mates
Mikey elly dog your now at those pearly gates
You've joined some other really great guys
Keep looking over us from the sky's

I hope you are now at peace
But you have left a empty space
Not up their but here on earth
You will be missed can't replace your worth

Rest in peace Elly dog
Save a place round the burning log
Pull up some sandbags and have a natter
About all things that don't really matter

You were a legend in your own right
Truly be missed your star shines bright
I hope you have found your peace
But no more mention of Barnet please

RECOVERY

I'm sure that I will survive
The answer soon will arrive

I am totally confused
Then again minds not amused

In the deep pits of despair
The family show they care

I cannot grab the sharp knife
That's won't be fair on my wife.

I must remain tall and strong
The truth is that I belong

In the fortress of my fear
The strange voices I do hear

I will beat the nasty thought
The skills that I have been taught

I'm amazed how far I've come
The thoughts have begun to run

I will stay on this journey

That is part of recovery!!!

REMEMBRANCE 2022

As Remembrance approaches this year
Many an adult will shed a tear
2022 and casualties still fall
Servicemen struggling to stand tall

We think it's all about two world wars
In reality it is about many many tours
Those that fell in foreign lands
We remember with marching bands

Boots, medals and uniform done
Stand on parade wait for the drum
March of at a 30 inch pace
Remember it is not a race

You don't have to be on the parade
Just remember the sacrifices that were made
Bow you head as the last post is played
Reflect and remember those who were paid

It doesn't matter if you never served
Two minutes silence must be observed
While it's quiet have a look around
Those with medals have been on the ground

The ultimate fear , is the not coming back
In a Draped coffin with a union jack
Those that are left can struggle after war
For their absent friends during the tour

Friday 11th is tomorrow's date
Go to church and don't be late
If you can't make it to the service
At 11am don't be nervous

Stand in silence for two minutes
Remembrance has no limits
Stand with them and have this though
We owe our lives to those who fought

World War 1 and world war 2
The start of the poppy symbol is true
The blood that was spilt on Flanders fields
Did not stop others to yield

Many other wars caused death and destruction
Listen to this simple instruction
Respect those that have done their time
And remember those that are still on the line

Rest in peace all those from the past
You gave your lives to early and fast
We will remember you not just today
Remembrance has to be every day.

HRH QUEEN ELIZIBETH II R.I.P

The 8th of September twenty twenty two
A day of sad news is brought to you
London Bridge has fallen this was said
At eighteen thirty two Queen Elizabeth II is dead

Her Royal Highness reigned for seventy years
Her subjects she'd blood, sweat and tears
The longest reigning monarch to ever have served
Mourning across the world will be observed

A Queen, a monarch and a mother of four
The only Queen to do your bit during the war
A granny of 8 and gan gan of 12
Being a great monarch you did delve

Born Elizabeth Alexandra Mary in April 26
To Prince Albert who became George VI
No-one knew you would become Queen
The first decade of life being pristine

In 1936 uncle Edward abdicated the crown
Your whole world just turned upside down
Your first radio broadcast at the age of 14
"God will care for us and give us victory"

Your first inspection of troops in 1942
Pragmatic and kind but that's what you do
In 1945 you did your bit for the war effort
Joining the ATS as a mechanic and driving expert

In 47 you married your childhood sweetheart
Very seldom was it you were ever apart
Your true resilience again was shown
As you collected fabric coupons for your gown

In 1948 your first son charles was born
Then came Anne whom I've met on the lawn
Ten year later Andrew did come
Two years later Edward your youngest son

In February 52 your father did pass
You became Queen as a 24 year old lass
June 53 the your coronation year
First one broadcasted caused many a tear

In the 70 years you did so much
The commonwealth you kept in touch
Your political views almost always hidden
Even recently meeting president Bidden

Stiff upper lip and done what's right
Keeping the family together a real fight
You are now on your final journey
Together forever with Philip and corgis

You will be missed as Commander in Chief
I thought this poem was going to be brief
From all your citizens on all your land
We shout out loud Liz was grand

R.I.P your Majesty
God's Speed
Forever eternity.

THE WIND BLOWS HAIKU

See the trees blowing

The wind across your face blows

The rain will arrive

R.I.P DEAN

We lost a good guy within the last week
Name of Dean Parry Val halla did seek
A full military career this gentleman had
His family and friends are now very sad

We've known Dean since the age of sixteen
When we joined a life in green
A top soldier and tradesman for sure
Serving abroad in many a war

Tomorrow's the day he'll be laid to rest.
From all of us you were one of the best
The current climate won't let us attend
But we will raise a glass for this absent friend

You join Andy perks at the bar in the sky
Leaving us behind wondering why
We know about demons that you had
Now they are gone and you can be glad

Our condolences to your family
I hope it goes well. as well as can be
R.I.P Dean Respect to thee.
From all the reprobates of 87C

Champion Squadron
Champion Recruit troop
1st Sept 87

STRUGGLING MIND

I'm feeling so sad
Am I that bad
I cannot handle any stress

Locked in a cage
Full of this rage
It truly is a mess

Nothing seems right
My chest feels tight
What's wrong is anyone's guess

It's not good for my health
Reach for the tablets on the shelf
The idea is not the best

Grounding techniques applied
I have nowhere to hide
It's not easy I must confess

Feeling so alone
These thoughts have grown
I cannot lay and rest

The black dog is strong
I hope not for long
But now I do digress.

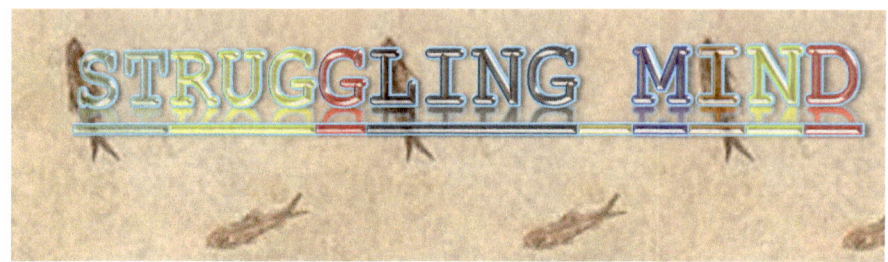

100 YEARS ON

One hundred years ago in 1921
The 15th of May a new charity began
Amalgamating charities of which there were 4
The Royal British Legion set up to aid those from the great war.

Earl Haig and Tom Lister were the founders.
Supporting those back from Flanders
1.75 million of those that returned
Had some form of disability from amputee or minds totally burned

Then there were those wives, widow's daughters and sons.
Who's Husbands, Fathers lives had succumbed
Their lives taken by the enemy
The RBL emblem became the Flanders poppy

The poppy is the symbol of Remembrance
For the sacrifice of life, so peace had a chance
Every conflict since the great war
More recently Afghanistan, Iraq, some more obscure

Korea, Malaya, Oman and The Falklands
Servicemen and women put lives in others hands
So commemorate their passing on Armistice day
11th November sit quietly and pray

Without these sacrifices in all these wars
The world would have broken that's for sure
So every year stand still and reflect
Those that died deserve your respect

Those that survived may be stood in your town
Looking sorrowful and feeling down
The best thing you can do is show your support
Words from Brigadier Marriot " Do as you ought"

Bow your head when you hear that bugle play
Stand still and watch those on parade this Remembrance Day
Someone in your family`s history
Will have been effected by a catastrophe

Join in be proud of your countries past
Hopefully all these sacrifices are finished at last
But if not, and more wars happen
Support those military men and women

They have no choice whether to stay or go
Orders are followed, allegiance they show
For Queen and country they will fight
For your freedom and human right.

Remember them is all I say.

For your Tomorrow they gave their today!!!

D DAY 80 YEARS ON

Some came by air
Some came by sea
They fought and died
So we could be free

The 6th of June 1944
Normandy a place in France
Operation Overlord or Neptune
Thousands took their last stance

Parachutists and gliders and
boats of all size
Thousands of soldiers met their demise
156,115 allied soldiers took part this way
80 years ago on D DAY

The beaches to name a few were called
Omaha, Utah, Juno and Sword
The largest allied beach invasion to date
So many died because of fate

10,500 allied casualties in one day
Fought for our freedom all I can say
Respect, hats of sir where it's due
I and others will remember you

REMEMBER RESPECT

BIZZARE PTSD EXPERIENCE TODAY

A bizarre experience happened today
Went into flight mode all I can say
Felt I was followed paranoia set in
Couldn't rid the voices from deep within

Went to a shop and bought myself drink
Found a hidey hole so I could just sink
No one would find me now that's a shame
When it is over I feel no pain

My mind is mashed
Don't know where to turn
My thoughts are on fire
Just want them to burn

As I wallowed in my pit of despair
I realised that people did care
I pulled myself out of this dark hole
Felt I had failed deep in my soul

Today's a new day and feelings haven't gone
Try to convince myself I do belong
Grounding exercises aren't working one bit
Please help me out of this sorrowful pit

As I write this little poem
I've come back to this plain
It's because of requiem

Family and friends don't deserve pain!!!

YOU BELONG

You belong
Stay strong

Fight the demon within
You know you can win

Shed a tear
You are here

Live life to the full
You are no fool

Fight or Flight
Do what's right

32 VETERANS PASSED SO FAR

32 have taken their own lives.
Leaving behind, children, friends and wives
How much longer is this to go on
Devastating families is totally wrong

No person should get to this state
When they could just chat to a mate
Asking for help is not a sign of weakness
It's about sharing your bleakness

Other ways to cope with this mess
Admit that you are in distress
Learn about breathing, and using your senses
This will strengthen your defences

That black dog that sits on your shoulder
Let it know you were a soldier
You are strong and can't be beat
You are not ready for defeat

My ask is that everyone shares
To show all affected somebody cares
This is not a massive ask
Go and see them take a flask

Sit down with a listening ear
Let them know you are here
Have a chat and make a brew
Chew the fat like you use too

Being beside them is really great
The true meaning of a mate
If you do this simple thing
You could stop heavens bar-bellring

Two of Our Own

Two of our have gone missing today
Two guys from the corps sad to say
The demons they have are very strong
Let's get these guys back where they belong

This is happening more frequently now
Veterans going missing Why? How?
Something more needs to be done
The battles they have, haven't been won

More care and funding would be a start
From society then they could feel a part
They are not weird, strange or odd
They are veterans part of a squad

Removed from their familiar surrounds
An alien country there in with unwanted sounds
But no it is home they are at
Not feeling normal how'd you fancy that

Panic attacks and unwanted dreams
No normality here or so it seems
They say be strong stand and fight
You can't see the enemy it's time for flight

The enemy is not in far off lands
It's in the head eating out of your hands
They don't know what to do for the best
Anxiety depression burning their chest

Sadly one of the guys did pass
The other still confused in the grass
He cannot see the love all around
He just wants to be on the ground

I hope this chap is found safe soon
He really needs help to find his moon
His family and friends are worried sick
This young man needs a gentle kick

Get home young soldier your family await
Find the love you deserve lose all the hate
You are a veteran now please stand tall
No more veterans need to fall

R.I.P Jak I didn't know you at all
I feel great sadness that you did fall
My condolences to family and friends
Hope they find comfort as your pain ends

This shouldn't happen in this great land
They should grow old hear marching bands
But alas I know it always will be
Until funding is found can't they see.

RIP MARK TAFF LANGLEY

Devastated at the news I've heard.
Totally shocked this is absurd
The passing of a Welsh legend
Proud to have served my butty friend.

He started his long career
As a proud Welsh infanteer
He then transferred to the Corps
His knowledge he used that's for sure

I first met Taff in the Adriatic
In a place we all called FRY
Former Republic of Yugoslavia
For those that don't know why

Taff was known to do silly things
But one that comes to mind
Being pumped up a scam 12
Blind just leading the blind

He earned a commendation whilst in Afghanistan
As multiple commander he looked after every man
A real genuine gentle man who liked a practical joke
His favourite tipple was vodka and coke

The next verse is for you
Reading from above
I hope it hits a chord baloo
Also for those that you love

Gwneud hyn yn Gymraeg i chi er
fy mod i'n teimlo'n las eich calon
oedd calon y ddraig Gymreig
chwedl a pharagon

Doing this in welsh for you
even though I'm feeling blue
your heart was that of the welsh dragon
a legend and a paragon

I apologize now if my grammar is wrong
Like butty would say you f*****g mong
When you served you were a "RELAY"
Not one of god's chosen what can I say

The black dog was on his shoulder
I know It's a crap place to be
I'm gutted brother soldier
You didn't shout out to me

My condolences to the family
The brotherhood does feel your pain
R.I.P Brother Mark Langley
Until we meet again

So save all of us a seat at the bar.
With Tony, Mac, Ange, to name but a few.
You have left behind your family and friends
We all miss you!!!!

SERGEANT Mark (Taff) Langley
Royal Signals

1969 - 2021

FEELING SO DOWN

I just want to hurt myself
I just don't know why
My family's my world
Now I need to cry

This is so really bizarre
Feel like driving a car
I can't do that I've had a drink
Am I really on the brink

It's a dark place I'm sat in
Switch on the light
Let my life begin
I'm ready to fight

I've had a good day
and beaten the thoughts
Happy with all of my cohorts
But now it is night

the bad thoughts are strong
Trying to convince I dont belong
What is going on in my brain
I know I'm not really insane

A bit confused at this time
Fight it now get in line
It's really hard I must confess
My head says one thing
My heart says the rest

I need sleep that's for sure
Tomorrows the day I find a cure
After a little sleep I do wake cranky oh for goodness sake
The same feelings are in my head

Remain positive the counsellor's said
A new day begins so does grounding
I'm so down need to look at my surroundings
Listening to the chirps of the birds
Telling me not to be so absurd

Feeling the wind upon my face
I'm a member of the human race
The smells around me are so sweet
Brings me back to my feet

Take today as a new beginning
The new chapter of me winning
Black dog still sits on my shoulder
But hey I'm another day older

PTSD I DON'T WANT TO SLEEP

I know I'm really tired
I just don't want to sleep
I guess I'm just really wired
Dreams will make me weep

I'm scared to see those things and sounds
Locked deep inside my brain
Make me sweat and wriggle around
Makes me think that I'm insane

Rational thinking is the cure
Its easier said than done
When your thoughts are so obscure
Rationality is to far gone

Stay awake with my relief
Is the action I shall do
My inner thought bare belief
Share them all with you

Anger resentment on oneself
Is a starter just for ten
Nice and calm me sat on the shelf
It's happening all too often

Guilt that burns within ones soul
Is hotter than volcano lava
Need to find the deepest hole
And cool it like a bottle of cava

Worthlessness is another one
But how can this be the case
For advice i give to everyone
But I can't keep up the pace

Failure is the biggest thing
It hits you like a rock
Needing help is so belittling
You want to crawl into a sock

I could of said an obscenity
In that last verse of course
But this I say with sincerity
I will get back on my horse

These feelings now I've let out
Are because I'm so upset
So I write in form or shout
To be in front of the net

Glad to be on this mortal coil
Walk head high once again
Get sleep at night with no spoil
Black dog inflict no pain

Goodnight "sleep well"

PTSD INSOMNIA

It's 10 pm I go to bed
Try to rest my weary head

It's 11 pm I just can't sleep
Things I'm seeing make me weep

It's 12 am I've drifted off
Woken again as I start to cough

Its 1 am I'm awake again
I don't need to see this pain

It's 2am I'm restless still
I get up take a pill

It's 3am I nod of once more
Bet I'm awake again at 4

It's 4 am I've had my snooze
I wonder if it's lack of booze

Its 5am I'm asleep at last
This sleeping game goes to fast

Its 6am I'm still sleeping tight
Then my memories start to fight

Its 7am I'm now wide awake
The alarm went off my mistake

It's 8am off to work I go
Hope it's quick not to slow

Its 10 am and I'm working hard
Even posted a birthday card

Its 12 pm and lunch break starts
I'm really tired falling apart

Its 1 pm didn't manage a nap
Think I need a night cap

Its 3 pm seven hours to push
Maybe I could lay under a bush

Its 5pm on my way home
I ring my family on the phone

Its 6pm it's family time
Before bed listen to rhyme

Its 7pm I'm totally shattered
Have tea then adults chattered

Its 8pm nearly time for bed
When I can rest my weary head

It's 9pm not long to wait
For my mind to take the bait

It's 10pm I take myself up
Feel like I'm in a thermos cup

Back in bed it starts over again
When will I sleep and see no pain

You're Not Useless

Am I really that useless?
That may not be the case
I am just another person
Within the human race

Everyone has problems
This I know is fact
It's how I deal with them they say
In other words, how do I react

Some peoples brains work differently
This I know to be true
The problems that some people have
May not affect me and you

To some normal stresses can be hard
They can see their way through
But to others with severe issues
These stresses cannot do

When the mind is struggling so much
You cannot see the way
Ideas bounce around your head
You can't hear what others Â say

No one has the answers
The mind is so complex
The smallest things will fester
In the minds deepest depths

Low self-esteem will set in
Negative thoughts do begin
Try to increase your self-belief
As if you don't it will cause grief

Some people can see the light
Where others just sit in fright
Others always see positive
Where some just don't want to live

A friend colleague a partner can listen
So shout out to achieve this mission
It's not the easiest thing to do
Once it's done you won't feel so blue

It's easy for others to just say
Get a grip be on your way
What you need is a listening ear
Fill your life with positive cheer

So if you're struggling and cannot see
You're not alone shout out too me
I'm no professional in this matter
As you are not mad as a hatter

I will listen to your worries and woes
Watch your movement from head to toe
As this will help me see what is wrong
Give you the answer that you belong

You deserve to let your mind be free
Give people a chance and you will se
Let them help you through your strife
You can then begin to live your life

SOLDIER F

Soldier F was charged today
Disgusted is all I can say
Doing a job in times gone by
Ask yourselves the reason why

Deployed there at the government's request
Where's your loyalty out of interest
He done what others wouldn't do
So your life today wouldn't be blue

Went over there on demand
On orders given by this land
To help the people who soon would hate
47 years on he meets his fate

The bog side in Derry is where this was
Protesters and rioters present for their cause
Petrol bombs and broken glass
What would you do is what I ask

Fight for your Country the posters did say
Don't let terrorists get in the way
Bring them to justice for atrocities carried out
Not the soldier who came to your shout

Now every soldier has done there bit
Showing true British grit
Not easy being on receiving end
Not knowing if enemy or friend

The bit that hurts those that have served
Unfair treatment not deserved
Soldier F should be let free
He did his bit for liberty

So judge and jury and public spirit
Open your eyes could you have done it
March amongst all the chaos and debris
To help those who want to be free

100 YEARS LEST WE FORGET

One hundred years since the end
No veterans left to befriend
A war that saw many losses
We now remember with poppy crosses

They fought in trenches side by side
Even fought as their comrades died
Over the top when the whistle blew
Hoping today, God was with you!

Through wire and craters and exploding shell
No man's land must have been hell
Keep marching on showing true grit
Hoping that you were not hit

A British Tommy with a gun
Fighting for freedom against the hun
Some were only in their teens
Seeing things that shouldn't be seen

Death and the use of mustard gas
How long did this war last
4 years 3 months and 14 days
Many soldiers learnt to pray

Over 8 million soldiers met their end
21 million injured or round the bend
250000 were too young to serve
This is not what children deserve

Fight for freedom they did delve
The youngest being a mere twelve
28 June nineteen fourteen
Catalyst for a war to begin

The assassination of Archduke Ferdinand
Creating unrest on this fair land
28 July war was declared
Between other countries but Britain cared

The Great War or World War One
This war in Europe would be long
From Tannenberg to Cambrai
Lots more battles I cannot lie

Many other battles during these years
Lots of fatalities and thousands of tears
I doth my hat to those that fell
For the younger generation this I tell

They gave their lives so you could live
For the poppy appeal spare change please give
The money goes to those who've served in need
No matter what colour, Religion or creed

Many wars have happened in the last 100 years
Millions and millions of people's tears

The poppy fund was created for this cause
To help every serviceman/women returning from wars

So in November on the eleventh day
At 11 A M bow your head and say
One simple word it's easy to do
That simple word is "THANKYOU"

https://unsplash.com/photos/red-petaled-flowers-during-golden-hour-CcRZ4k3c6gA?utm_content=creditShareLink&utm_medium=referral&utm_source=unsplash

HELP GIVE ME STRENGTH

HELP me I'm struggling today
These thoughts won't go away

Help me I feel so sad
Am I really that bad a dad

Angry at the slightest of things
Losing it when that bell rings

The bell that just can't be heard
So cranky it's really absurd

Help me I feel I have failed
Yet again my judgement is impaled

Help me get back on the road
I don't like this when I explode

Scary to the ones that I love
Here the calling of the white dove

Go away dove it's not my time
Leave me be and I'll be just fine

Venom of a deadly snake does alight
My family are the ones I do fright

I must now attempt to put it right
Stay awake late into the night

Force all these thoughts away
Live once more to fight the day

It came this time out of the blue
I really don't know what to do

Fight or flight is what I have learnt
Alas either way I will be burnt

Locked away to drown my sorrow
I need to find that tomorrow

But tomorrow is the thing that never arrives
Regret and sadness is what appears

Tears flow from these tired eyes
Not wanting to say goodbyes

The demon within is strong this time
Pulling hard on the twine

I'm using every ounce of strength I have left
But he knows I'm so bereft

If I go then he has won again
Taken another of mortal plain

But I'm not ready for an epilogue
I'm the Prince dressed as the frog

The love I get from my family
Give me strength and clarity

He is strong but I remain still
Win this battle yes I will

VICTORY

FIGHT OR FLIGHT

Fight or flight happened again today
Don't know why or what to say
Anger deep inside my mind
Not really seeing, feeling blind

So I went for a wander
To clear my head
Far over yonder
Here's what the voices said

Your better than this you are great
Get on the phone ring your mate
This is just one of them blips
Walk on son get outta them dips

The other voice telling me to quit
Making me feel like I should slit
Laughing loudly deep inside
This is when I sat and cried

It's not very easy knowing your wrong
But I had to remain strong
Anger, sadness is what I felt
Sat on the grass wanting to melt

I've survived worse this I know
Recovery may be really slow
I'm ready to fight this head on
Positive thoughts and staying strong

Don't just ask "how am I?"
Otherwise I will make you cry
The reason is I'm not good
Miss those lost from brotherhood

Listen to me and what I say
Empathize don't run away
I need your help this is for sure
Then together we'll find the cure

R.I.P GILL

Today we say goodbye to Gill
This surely is a bitter pill
A lively lady full of the beans
A cruel world so it seems

A kind hearted lady with lots of love
On her final journey up above
A mother of 4 to say the least
Head of the table at the feast

Witty, funny and caring to all
Enjoy life at the angels ball
Now all the pain you had has gone
Dance with the stars go on go on

A rainbow queen that you were
Brighter than bright what I hear
Life like dolls being your passion
Keeping them into fashion

Other things I know you love
Your grandchildren and daughters above
We'll all miss your thoughtfulness
Even things that made us blush

Your best friend feebie was your pooch
But definitely not Turner and hooch
Pampered dog with plenty of coats
Miss you on the rainbow floats

So look over us from up there
We all know you do care
When we want reasons why
We will just look up to the sky

Thankyou mum, granny for being you
Now you've gone we are all blue
Wish we could feel your gentle touch
We LOVE and MISS you so so much

PAIN

I feel so empty
I cannot cope
My friends are plenty
I just mope

I cannot cope
These thoughts in my head
Give me the rope
Wish I was dead

Hurt everything I ever touch
This I know about so much
Thoughts running through my brain
Why do I feel insane

I feel the pain as the blade penetrates
I wish I'd gone with my mates
Yes that's right I've lost good friends
Maybe now this is my end

I know it's a selfish thing
I can hear the angels sing
My mouths gone dry
I begin to cry

I can't cope anymore
Screwed up head that's for sure
Feeling of sadness and remorse
I am no Trojan horse

Empty, scared I feel weak
No wisdom left cannot speak
I'm sorry everyone I need to go
Those that know I now know

MENTAL HEALTH STIGMA

Mental health stigma within the military
Injuries you just can't see
Many sufferers have taken their own lives
Leaving behind families husbands and wives

In honour of those who ended their plight
It's time to show this isn't right
Awareness, look out for each other
Brothers and sisters from another mother

R.I.P all those gone before
With your passing opens the door
Mental health awareness is a must
Or your eyes will fill with dust

NOT A SIGN OF WEAKNESS

It's not a sign of weakness
Talking is the way to win
It may not take away the demon
Hold it at bay within

A brew a Natter may really help
Put these thought to one side
Social media is where you can yelp
Instant messenger we can confide

If it's a one on one you need
Then it's only a phone call away
Whatever time night or day
It's the right thing yes indeed

I know you may not want to bother
But bother it is not
A brother from another mother
That is what you got

So please don't do anything rash
I know your better than that
It's a fight to the finish not a dash
So put on your winners hat

Take notice from I who know
You can beat this nasty thought
Think of those around you now
Don't leave them all distraught

They love you, want you around
Hold on to that dear thought
Not visit you in the ground
In words I heard a long time ago
DO AS YOU OUGHT

Stay strong my friend
You're the best to really judge
It's not your time to call end
Don't make me hold a grudge

I hope you see what these words mean
Not trying to patronize
Your ace this is how your seen
Now open up your eyes

If I don't know you it's not the end
You too can take heed
Everyone has a special friend
Their your saviour yes indeed

R.I.P STEVE

In Tilshead I met a good guy
Unfortunately he has now gone
Taken to the angels in the sky
His name was Steve baron

A North Eastern lad that's for sure
A kind heart all so pure
Talented linguist speaking Pashtu
Your family and friends now miss you

A gunner was cap badge of choice
We will miss that Geordie voice
Saddened to hear about your demise
Look after us left from the skies

At last my friend you can rest
You've earnt your medals on your chest
Sleep tight big man demons are gone
Your legacy will live on

Condolences to friends and family
You've left a massive void
You'll always be a drop short Steve
Banter you can't avoid

R.i.p brother in that sky
I hope you hear the lullaby
No more noise for you young man
Angel music and a beer can

R.i.p Steve baron

PRESENCE OF THE ABNORMAL

Presence of the Abnormal
Is a sign to save your life
Presence of the normal
Keeps you out of trouble and strife

It's a sign to your inner soul
That protects you from being hurt
You just have but one goal
Keep your head out of the dirt

This happens in every life
It's something that can be beat
Believe in your senses and strive
Then you can walk along the street

Hold your head up high
If it doesn't feel right
Its not time to fly
It is the time to stand and fight

For you can get out of this place
Your senses have got you this far
Laugh in adversities silly face
You really don't need to go in that bar

As a child you had no fear
This is a way of life
As an adult these instincts disappear
You have troubles and plenty of strife

So, trust your mind and stay strong
The bad thoughts will diminish
On this world is where you belong
Your life is not ready to finish

GO AWAY SURVIVOR GUILT

Survivor guilt, is it in the head?
It feels like it's you that should be dead
Alas my friend this isn't so
This feeling needs to get up and go

For it will bring you to your knees
No one can hear you shout please
Go away survivor guilt
The life they need should be rebuilt

I know you are a demon in the brain
Bringing people all this pain
Lack of sleep is what you deprive
Let them move on with their lives

Survivors are what they have become
Your nothing but banging of a steel drum
Leave their soles to be content
Happiness is what is meant

So good bye guilt and sorrow
A new life begins tomorrow
Yes I know they've lost good people
But they'll meet again at the steeple

POPPABEAR

This poem is written for a mates dad
The family left feeling awfully sad
For their Poppabear passed this week
A better life he tries to seek

A Son, A Brother, A Father too
Your baby bears were very proud of you
Yes you had your demons with fags and the booze
Alas your taking your final cruise

You gave your children a better life than you had
That's why they are proud to call you dad
Your early days with your brother were difficult and hard
No contact from parents not even a card

But you stayed true to your word
Gave your children love that's not absurd
Even though you struggled with your health
Your love to the kids was better than wealth

As a former soldier and a guardsman too
I'm sure your send-off won't be all blue
As a Guardsman you will stand tall
Erect to the front you will not fall

A handsome and witty chap you were
Direct to the point that was for sure
As a man who didn't mince his words
Assertive and polite but did not curse?

So Poppa Bear you will be missed
Now your baby bears are getting Pxxxed
RIP DAD we loved you so much
A single white feather is all now we can clutch

REMEMBRANCE 2017

Remembrance day is here again
The country pays its respect
The veterans eyes show his pain
His head is bowed as he reflects

It's not just about the great war
Although this is where it started
Many other conflicts, mainly abroad
Remember those who have departed

There are many servicemen on parade
Marching with veterans who'd gone before
A Solemn day not just a masquerade
These guys and girls have been to war

So tell your children what this day means
It's not a carnival that it would appear
Explain that it's about loss of life
That it's OK to shed a tear

Remembrance day must live on
The story of the poppy retold
One day those soldiers will be gone
The poppy emblem will be sold

I hope that this never occurs
And our youth will keep it strong
I hope you read this and concur
Our history does belong

So this Sunday 11th of November
Go outside and see them march past
This is the time we remember
Fallen from the beginning to the last

From Flanders fields to desert plains
These veterans deserve our praise
Our freedom is what was gained
As they walked through the smoke and haze

The younger veteran has also done his share
This we cannot forget
His actions in war he must bare
Their stories untold as yet

When they are told you'll be amazed
At what they have seen and done
Opium plantations set ablaze
Your freedom and life he won

POSITIVE MENTAL ATTITUDE

Go for a walk to clear your head
Life's too short to stay in bed
When you're feeling really low
Get outside feel the wind blow

No matter what walk of life
People suffer with troubles and strife
It may be no job or money for rent
It may be you feel your life is spent

But hear this you can get through
Many others feel just like you
It's all about occupying the mind
Staying strong the answers you'll find

But most of all don't keep it within
As this is truly a mortal sin
It will eat you up take away your strength
So find someone and talk at length

Positive mental attitude needed
You're a human not inbreeded
Focus on the small things first
Otherwise your mind will burst

LONDON TUBE EXPLOSION 2017

Another explosion in London today
When will they learn to go away?
General public hurt yet again
These terrorists are a real big pain

Setting off a device in a public place
You're no member of the human race
Hurting people doing their daily chores
You certainly won't get any applause

I hope all those hurt are on the mend
To these people this message we send
Don't let them change your daily routine
Report to the police anything you have seen

I send my thoughts to you all
Hope your families and friends can stand tall
Hope you're all healing and getting well
These nasty people will be sent to hell

Islamic state have claimed its their doing
What they need is a real good shoeing
No matter what you want to achieve
Your act of violence I can't believe

We will catch you and you will be sent to rot
In a 6 foot cell you will wish you were shot
Go back under the rock whence you came
Your spiteful acts they are evil and insane

Each day your strength will overcome
And you won't feel totally outdone
Finally believe you are really strong
Life challenges can do you no wrong

BARCELONA

Another terrorist atrocity has happened again
This time it was Barcelona and that my friends is Spain
My heart felt love goes to those affected
These terrorists need found and dejected

Stay alert everyone they may strike anywhere
Be vigilant and stay aware
They have hit London and Paris
They call themselves ISIS

They have tried to install fear to us all
But they're the only ones who will fall
They will not win their religious fight
Peace and tranquillity that's what is right

There tactics have been very similar
Killing, hurting with a van or a car
Driving at speed in built up areas
Targeting innocent bystanders

These people really are cowardly
I just wish that they would see
They have been totally brain washed
Reasons and thoughts turned to slosh

Sending healing thoughts to all people there
From the western world we really care
The terrorist should be behind a large fence
For indiscriminate acts of murder and violence

You are the scurvy of this earth
Your radical beliefs buried under turf
You cannot see that you won't win
What you do is really a Sin

So ISIS we won't take it anymore
Face up to facts you've lost your war
Go back home and leave our shores
Violence and murder we don't adore

ALCOHOL CAN NUMB THE PAIN

Alcohol can numb the pain
But it's not the best thing for it
So have a drink and have some fun
But please don't overdo it.

It's can be so addictive
You may need it everyday
But when you finally sober up
Your problems haven't gone away

Some say it is in your genes
Others say it's just being weak
Either way it is an addiction
It's help, and advice you really seek

Lifelong abuse will destroy
Everything you ever had
When your health deteriorates
Your family will be sad

I'm not saying don't have a drink
It's safe in moderation
But drinking vodka at breakfast
Won't get you admiration

Liver failure heart conditions
Symptoms you may get
To many people gone before
Some you've never met

Alcoholism is hard to beat
It's a drug that's legalized
If you keep drinking like you do
Your internals will be fried

Family and friends are there for you
To help you beat this sordid addiction
You will then realize, alcohol kills
This is FACT not fiction

ALCOHOL may temporarily numb the pain, but it will ultimately make things much, much worse.

SOBRIETY may temporarily be uncomfortable, but it will ultimately make things much, much better.

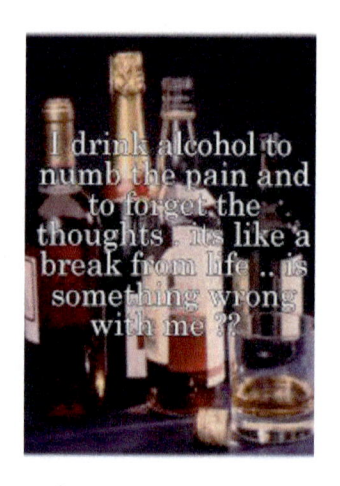

I drink alcohol to numb the pain and to forget the thoughts .. its like a break from life .. is something wrong with me ??

MENTAL HEALTH EPISODE

An episode may come and go
When it will come you will never know
From the left or right or head on
The way to beat it is to stay strong

Emotions and thoughts they run wild
Sometimes you just wish you were a child
Stay strong and try to remain upbeat
Keep yourself on your feet

Find someone whom you can talk
Or find a place to go for a walk
Clear your head and find that space
Only you know your safe place

Fight or flight is in the mind
If you run that would be unkind
Stand tall and fight the demon within
This is the only way you can win

Head on they say is the only way
To put these thoughts to bed one day
It won't just happen over night
This will be one long fight

But when you're feeling on top of your game
You will win and no more pain
Keep those you love close and near
They will help rid you of the fear

Sadness, loneliness feeling of remorse
Guilt, Anger and pain of course
Some of the feelings you may get
Waking up in the night soaking wet

These dreams you're having
Keeping you awake
Positive thoughts you need
For your own sake

Happy times that make you smile
Will help you through this last mile
When it rears its ugly head
Remember what this poem said

Stay strong, remain calm
You can win
What happened to you
Is not a sin

You are worth your weight in gold
Shout out and let the world be told
What you have encountered is truly sad
You're an amazing lady or lad.

MANCHESTER ATTACK

Yet another incident has happened today
When will these terrorists go away
Manchester this time at a concert
Some taken to early some really hurt

Their war now affecting the general public
These people are just really sick
To target young children having fun
Your sick and something will be done

You will not scare us of British decent
Your cowardly acts you must repent
We will hunt you down and take you in
A six foot cell your life will begin

Prayers go to all those that were there
Great British people show that you care
For those that have lost I shed a tear
Defeat this terrorism show no fear

Stay alert and watch each other's backs
We can beat these cowardly attacks

HELP WITH A LISTENING EAR

It's so not right
I wonder why
It's the dark of night
I begin to cry

I'm not in pain
From work today
Am I insane
Thoughts please go away

I'm normally an upbeat chap
Full of the joys of spring
Then memories come and give a slap
I just don't know where to begin

I know it will last for a few days
Hold me back and not let me think
Like one of those Broadway plays
No washing and cleaning make me stink

As they came out to haunt me
The memories are not very kind
All I need is some friendly company
To push them to the back of my mind

A chat and a good listening ear
Will pull me though this chapter
When I'm back and have no fear
Sit and wait for the next disaster

It is a cycle within the brain
That brings me to my knees
All I want is to drive and train
Think of the birds and bees

Mental health or crazy man
It's what your called by others
Affect anyone yes it can
Even you your sisters and brothers

Spare a thought for anyone you see
Who appears in distress
Listen to his words you may even disagree
Listening to this person is definitely the best

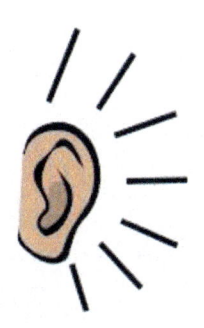

WORLD WAR 1 THE GREAT WAR

When they joined some were sixteen
In the war of 1914 to 18
They were young and gave their life
Some not even able to get a wife

They all joined for what was right
Freedom and humanity being their fight
Their basic training was not very long
Their bayonets were at least a foot long

They were trained hard and taught how to fight
Told they would live if they got it right
But this was false and the war went on
Mustard gas and tanks came along

Over the top when that whistle blew
What laid ahead no one knew
Wire entanglements and craters smoke all around
Explosions, gunfire and shouts of help the sound

Keep moving forward as best they could
Step over the wire and the burning wood
Pinned down by the enemy by that gun
Thinking of home that this is not fun

Sat in there foxhole looking for a way out
Rounds whizzing past hear another shout
Grenade is the call and then a large bang
Then you hear metal on metal clang

Gas is the next thing they hear shout
Quick quick pull that mask out
As the smoke goes over they lay and wait
Constantly checking on their mate

All clear all clear is now the order give
Their still here and are really driven
Back to the their trench they have to go
Stepping over bodies of friends and foe
This goes on until 1918
The eyes give away some sights they have seen
That spritely young man who went away
Not the same man who came back that day

Alas there are none of these hero's left
Families still sad and feeling bereft
Remember these men and others who follow
Without them we would have no tomorrow.

AM I PTSI OR PTSD

I am not good memories
I am not very kind
I am your history
Stuck in your mind

If you let me break you I must
Turn your life into dust
For I am your past etched into your brain
I will play back again and again

When you are low and cannot really think
I will appear try and make you sink
When I have you in my beastly net
Make it harder for help to get

I know your pride won't let you talk
From me I know you just can't walk
Because if you did you would feel shame
That is why I would win this game

Who am I, I hear you ask
I'm on your face I am your mask
I've had many names but I can't die
My newest one is PTSI

It's not just military I do this too
It's anybody who lets me even you
Everyone has a visit from me
In times of trauma or catastrophe

If this event happens in your time
I will help you now in this rhyme
You must talk about your experience
Then you will grow in confidence

If you are strong I cannot win
All bad thoughts go in the bin
A close network of friends will help with that
Talking laughing having a chat

Try and stay away from the pills
As this could lead to just more bills
Causing more stress and worry
Stay strong seek help there is no hurry

I will always be there to try again
So again stay strong fight your pain
You don't want me in your life
As I said I only cause strife

Signed **PTSI/PTSD??**

CBT THERAPY

There are people with this condition
And many people are not aware
This is not mental sub division
Join me and show you care
They suffer from sleepless nights
But they are not insomniacs
They remember flight or fight
Join me and have their backs

I raise awareness for their souls
To keep them feeling strong
Get shot of all there evil trolls
Keep these people where they belong
It's a condition known as PTSD
I want you all to understand
This can affect you and me
Or even someone in the school band

It is not just the serviceman or woman
That this can hurt and destroy
It's everyone on this land
From the eldest to youngest boy
It is the trauma that they have seen
That eats and niggles away
From accidents where they have been
Their memories are here to stay

These people need love and understanding
A shoulder, an ear or a friendly face
CBT is really outstanding
And is ahead in this race
For those that don't know what it is
Cognitive Behavioural Therapy
It's big words now understand this
It helps people to be happy

It gives them systems to understand
Attempts to conquer all their fears
Trains the mind to help them stand
Amongst emotion and the tears
It gives them hope
Gets them off the dope
Gives them a mission
And a vision

This is not a quick fix
Many demons will change tact
Be there for them in the mix
This will help that's a fact
Hope defeats suicide
It helps you to believe
This is going to be a hard ride
But they deserve to live

IT'S A BAD CONDITION

For everything I've seen and done
Nothing will compare
Soldiers taking their own live every week
This surely is not fair

They were trained to the highest degree
British soldiers pride is the best
Unfortunately governments disagree
And let them be laid to rest

If they had helped these soldiers out
Veterans wouldn't scream and shout
Something better needs to be done
Or unnecessary deaths will just go on

The UK is not alone it's happening across the pond
But one thing veterans always have is that military bond
So come on politicians do what is right
Spend money on after care and not just the fight

I know there are things like TRIM
While the soldier is away
But does this really help him
When living day to day

CBT is the way to go
Coping mechanisms put in place
So his mind can but grow
Demons come in last place

I know they have to shout for help
This shouldn't be the case
More support given before they yelp
And not just in their Base

They are not mental
They are not weak
Support is instrumental
An understanding what they seek

No nightmares if they do sleep
Hypersensitivity all but gone
The feeling of dropping into the deep
Is not where they belong

They deserve the help that they need
Written in the soldiers creed
Support and wellbeing is a must
So come and join stop being unjust

BAD WEEK ABSENT FRIENDS

The Corps has lost many this year
Many of us have shed a tear
Some from illness and mental health
Wish the grim reaper would lose his stealth

He sneaked up on these good men
To heaven he has taken them
For they were good people this is true
Please don't let the next be you

He's a crafty reaper this one
Taking people who should live on
In this last week he's taken three
This certainly should not be

From Tony to Dave and then PJ
I wish he would just go away
I know it's fact people die
It doesn't help us left to cry

These were members of The Royal Corps
Who had survived many a war
Communications was there game
The Signals Family won't be the same

To the families of these good men
My heart and condolences I do send
It will not help you in your grief
But remember faith and belief

So my brothers and sisters raise a glass
To absent friends who's lives did pass
I know people have to go
Rest in peace CERTA CITO

DIVORCE

When you think your world has ended
You feel you can't go on
There's people you have befriended
Will help you to become strong

Your marriage has just failed
It's nothing you have done
You have not been impaled
Man up and soldier on

This is just one challenge of life
The joker has thrown at you
She was just your lady wife
Now go and find number two

It may be money or loss of love
Or infidelity either side maybe
Any of these reasons mentioned above
There are many But I have only cited three

I'm not saying divorce is right
But happiness certainly is
It's better not to stand and fight
When the love has gone a miss

Many may say it can get costly
That is very true
Memories can be very ghostly
Erase the ones that make you blue

Keep everything in perspective
Keep your head held high
Don't let others who are so negative
Let you break and cry

Keep positive people around you
You will win this little war
Move forward this you really must do
Happiness in your hands now open that new door

And move along with your new life
And learn from your past
Maybe get your new wife
And this time hopefully it will last

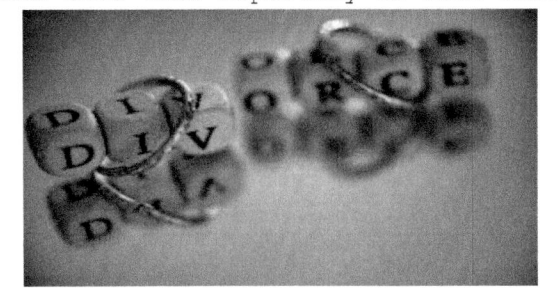

R.I.P TONY

Another sad day for the Corps
At the passing of a good lad
A loving husband
A fantastic dad

Airborne blood running through your veins
Leading from the front pulling those reins
Inspiring your men to do their best
A true gent and friend I do not jest

A real pleasure to have served with you
In Blandford and Elmpt to name but a few
I knew you as Geordie on our class 1
Now that was a course we had great fun

Pride and teamwork some values you had
Jumping out of planes you were mad
On terra firma football was your game
The Corps team won't ever be the same

Condolences go out to family far a wide
A true legend just cannot hide
Up in heaven looking over us
Keeping calm saying what's the fuss

Stand easy Tony your pain is gone
Your legacy of life will go on
As this poem comes to an end
I raise a glass for a strong leader and friend

Certa Cito

HOMELESS VETERAN

I served my country for the queen
When I left bad things I have seen
My life was turned upside down
People look at you with a disgusting frown

They did not know what I had done
A few years ago I carried a gun
On the streets I did live
Begging for money off people who would give

Pain I felt everyday
Wishing it would go away
I hit the drink and the drugs
So I couldn't feel the bugs

Finding the place to lay my head
Every night wishing I was dead
Find a cardboard box or a doorway
if you haven't done it you've nothing to say

It's a rough world on the streets
Fighting begging to make ends meet
I didn't realise people out there
The brotherhood really do care

I was lucky someone found me
Picked me up of my broken knee
Gave me a bed and not just rugs
They supported me of the drugs

And now that I'm on the way
Taking it day by day
I must really thank my friends
Now that past life is at end

REMEMBER

That time of year has come again
When we reflect and remember them
Polish our boots and press our kit
Remember those fallen that didn't make it

We shine our medals
Place them on our chest
Remember our friends
We have laid to rest

Remember those that went before
Those that were lost in another war
People think it's for soldiers old
Now it's time for them to be told

Rightly so we should do it with pride
Mark of respect for them that died
Show the world they didn't die in vain
For their families I feel the pain

They fought for our freedom of speech
And died on a foreign beach
Yes I'm talking about Dunkirk
And you may think I'm berserk

Without these acts of soldiers past
Would we be here and talk so fast
So on this day in mid-November
I ask you all to sit and remember

The 11th hour on the 11th day
Shall be known as armistice day
When we wear a Flanders poppy
And some of us may get soppy

It is good to let the tears flow
It shows gratitude to those that know
So as you see me March past
I was a soldier and not the last

There are veterans in there early twenties
Who stand tall and tears are plenty
Bravery and courage may appear less
No whistle blows but I digress

The point of this is to say
If only war would go away
These men and women have survived
Some of them burning up inside

So remember the fallen that is right
Bear a thought for servicemen tonight
And all those veterans on parade
Bow your head as they have stayed
R.I.P all personnel who have passed
CARPE DIEM

CAREING FOR PTSD SUFFERER

It comes in many shapes and forms
Some from abuse some from wars
Others include accidents or death
One thing is real they are all bereft

I'm talking about ptsd in remission
Anyone can suffer from this condition
It is always there in the mind
Helpless lonely feeling blind

To help these people you must be strong
Sometimes it's tiring and days are long
Be there for them when they call
To you it may appear so small

Give them a hug if there are down
If there tears are flowing don't just frown
Listen to them as their fears unfold
Pull up your chair as experiences are told

Once they've spoken do not mock
There mind is ticking like a cuckoo clock
If you do they may implode
Or worst still totally explode

What they need is a reason to live
You are the power and need to give
Don't condescend and say normal stuff
It will be ok is not enough

Find something they can grab hold
A purpose in life that can't be sold
A feeling of an accomplishment is a must
A lot to give and gain there trust

Once this hurdle has been broken
Many other things will be spoken
Listen intently and offer advice
Whatever you do don't patronise

If you struggle and can't complete
Liaise with a charity who you can meet
They will help you save this friend
Ptsd is a killer and that needs to end

Mental Health Hurts

Mental health issues are a horrible thing
Make you think life's not worth living
You learn to hide your inner thoughts
Even from all your cohorts

You just don't know where to turn
Every emotion makes you burn
But deep inside your really nice
The issues you've faced you pay the price

There is help out there you cannot see
But if you want talk to me
I'm not a doctor I will not judge
My mind is blank just like fudge

I know you feel you're going insane
But you're not it's your inner brain
If you talk, you will feel better
Hopefully get off that helter-skelter

Stand tall and fight this inner ghoul
For you are strong and not a fool
Don't think it's easy to just end
Think of your family and your friend

They will always be there for you
They are hurting very much too
But they need you to understand
They want you here, beside you they stand

Ptsd Or Battle Shock

The problem of having PTSD
is no one can see your injury

You may be vacant and just stare
Others think you just don't care

The demons are their day and night
Wanting you to flee or fight

Nowhere to run too you must stand
Fight your fears hand to hand

You just can't sleep the dreams hurt your brain
You bang your head thinking your insane

You know you need help from others around
They don't understand they weren't on the ground

Anxious and scared is another issue
But please don't grab a paper tissue

It is not pity that we seek
It is help as life appears so bleak

Family and friends try their best
But to them you're a total mess

You hit the drink and maybe the drugs
Pick at your skin get rid of the bugs

Governments sent you to faraway land
Now it appears they've washed their hands

I don't know if this is strictly true
But I do know they needed you

Some may say we were just a number
But it's not our fault were in this slumber

The places we went the things we saw
Another type cast "casualty of war"

So if you know of someone like this
Be supportive ptsd is hard to miss

They will say that they are ok
But say no and go out of your way

It will be appreciated trust me you'll see
They will turn it around and agree

You pulled them out of that dark place
And to heaven's door it will be last place

Lee Dodgeson Rip

R.I.P Lee Alan Dodgson
29 Feb 1976 - 12 Sept 2016

Another sad day has come to light
One of our mates has lost his fight
It's hard to say goodbye to a brother
Even if it's from another mother

Lee or dodge known by his mates
I hope it's ok at those pearly gates
You're going to be missed that's for sure
By all who served with you in war

Dodge I know you had a rough ride
And there are others with you on that side
Get to the bar and pull up a pew
Keep looking down on us few

Your family miss you and it's not right
From early morning to late at night
I for one am deeply upset
For the loss of a great guy I had once met

A legend when working on the 43s
A real worker easy to please
Pleasure to have served with thee
From the desert rats to the mighty 3

I now know you are at peace
Away from the demons or even the police
There's lots of other things I could say
But they will just get in the way

I great soldier that is true
Many people left feeling blue
Football and family your real passion
Didn't like your sense of fashion

Rest in peace my armoured friend
Until we meet at the clouds end

Angela Kay Rip

Corporal Angela (Ange) Birgit Kay
28July 1985 29 April 2015

I Met this girl in 2011
But alas she has gone to heaven
She was a great girl
And a Yorkshire lass

Far too young
For her too pass
When we were down
Ange was there

Now for your family
We send this prayer
A daughter a Sister
A fiancé and friend

But we all know
It's not the End
You have now gone
To see others past

In our minds
You will always last
Football was but one passion
And so was Tug o War

A real talent representing the Corps
A true spirited girl who
Strived for the best
Now you can be laid to rest

Ange you will sure be missed
Up in heaven getting Pxxxed
Look after those that went before
And remember it's not a chore

Rip our dear Ange
Even if we called you flange
It was a pleasure to have served with you
Even now I'm feeling blue

You were the best a friend could ask for
Please save us a place at heaven's door
Until that day we meet again comes
Fly with those angels in the sky

And let us worry about the Why
R.I.P Angela Kay gone too young

911 15th ANNIVERSARY

Fifteen years have passed
Since that fatal day
When terrorists killed 343
This is what it means to me

The people going about their day
Passengers flying on their way
Evil men take over the plane
Fly into the building that's insane

The losing of all those innocent
No way they can repent
I know it was done for their cause
But all its done is create wars

From this major catastrophe
Many people just don't see
people have suffered from nightmares and the loss of life
Terrorist should be locked up for causing all this strife

My heart goes out too those that lost
Family and their friends
And wish that this event could be labelled the means towards the end
They will not be forgotten

As it changed the world that day
Everyone feeling rotten
Hands in my head I pray
I am not a religious man

One thing I must just say
Look Mr terrorist take it
And please go away
The world does not need this trouble
It's been going on too long
To many people hurt in the rubble

Forget your radicalisation and move along
Rest in peace everyone
Affected by the act
Let's hope the leaders of the world
Can sit and make a pact

PTSD PRESSUP CHALLENGE

The 22 press up challenge is a real good thing
It helps the sufferer see that people do care
Without this challenge they couldn't sing
But it's all about making people aware

Ptsd is a horrible fate
In all walks of life Suffered by many
But please understand to lose a mate
Is far too much for any

I'm not saying go out and do
It's a challenge to make people see
It's for people like me and you
All it is 22 press-ups easy

The thing these people have seen and done
Should never be witnessed by anyone

#22PushUpChallenge

donate £5 by texting PTSD22 to 70004

COMBAT STRESS
THE VETERANS' MENTAL HEALTH CHARITY

REST IN PEACE YOUNG SOLDIER

Rest in peace fellow soldier
Your time here is done
When your family are much older
A family member and a son

You gave your life for us all
For the lives that we may lead
You are now attending heavens ball
About you, generations they will read

Your sacrifice is not wasted
This I can assure
This poem is not cut and pasted
It's about every death in war

You will be missed by many a friend
And family that's a fact
I bow my head in the end
As I too did take the pact

Although I'm here to tell my tale
It hurts me every day
When family's all go very pale
When the bugle has to play

PTSD LIFE

P̲resence of unwanted dreams.
T̲remors in my body it causes
S̲earching for answers it would seem
D̲angerous as there are no pauses

L̲oving oneself is hard to create
I̲ntimacy is so far away
F̲riendship begging I need a mate
E̲nergy depletes every day

WAR IN A VIEW

I don't like to talk about politics
And defiantly not religion
But listen world this makes us sick
Love and peace is what should be given

Politicians make the decision
To do what they think is right
Send forces off to faraway lands
Give mandates for them to fight

People sometimes are not nice
In the countries I have been
But maybe they should've thought twice
Could they cope with what I've seen

Some say this is for the great of god
But this is not always the case
Religious belief taken into account
That country is their place

I know we do a damn fine job
Many lives have been saved
But really world is it right
Too many early graves

The government of the day
Need to listen to the people
Political views and religious ways
Cause death and visits to the steeple

FAMILY

Family starts generations before
Some of whom have served in the war
Some are still here some are gone
But hear this love goes on

Your parents are the first you see
Perched up upon there crooked knee
Then siblings come into the mix
New best friends to pick up sticks

As you get older you meet your lady
And together you then have a baby
This is the start of your own tree
As you sit your baby next to thee

Tenderness love and understanding
Will give your children a good grounding
Love your children though everything
Even when they do sin

They are yours you can't deny
Give them love before they fly
It will help them in the end
The meaning of family is our best friends

INSPIRATION

I sit and reflect
New words help me to connect
Signs from above come to me
Poet I would like to be
Informative i like to write
Rhyme and reason is so bright
Always try to be just so
Testing my words do they flow
In this style is my first plight
Only you can say if it's right
Now I must say goodnight

I WAS A SOLDIER

I was a soldier of the past
And I know im not the last
I signed up to serve my Queen
Far off lands I have seen

As that soldier I done my best
Losing friends laying them to rest
We fought for what was only right
Giving freedom to others at night

As bullets flew and bombs exploded
Â My thoughts and mind just imploded
I could not say I wasn't scared
But my vision was not impaired

The smell of cordite all around
Waiting for the alarm to sound
Then the order of stand fast
Hoping this attack would not last

They come at us with all they have
Rpgs and a Gustav
We hold firm and do not falter
It's not our turn at the alter

Be brave young man I have to shout
As the young man does scream out
I've been hit this is bad
I wish I was with my mum and dad

It's ok you will be fine
It's a promise that is mine
The bombardment ends and we look up
Let's sort this out my young pup

Gingerly we give first aid
That is why we get paid
We stretcher him out to the Heli pad
In a few days he's with mum and dad

After a while I go to see
That young soldier who laid before me
He's up and about and full of cheer
Winks at me we go for a beer

For those guys that didn't survive
We raise a glass cuddle and cry
For all the new guys on your career
Wish you well I got your ear.

Up the Hill

I went up the Kiwi to see the tree
It was Mike Parke I went to see
We had a chat and put the world to rights
And yes we established I'm too old to fight

Sat up there on the hill
I really saw what was the thrill
The view you have is truly amazing
In the distance the sheep are grazing

Mike your legacy lives on
A true gent with a beautiful son
Kady has really done you proud
I just wish you were still around

You touched the hearts of all you met
Even when you made us sweat
I feel for your family as you have gone
But like I say you legacy goes on

Thanks again Mike for all you have done
In life and even now when you have gone
You are a star and truly missed
And before you say no I'm not p####d

Thank you for you chat today
Made it clearer
Showed me the way
In your debt I will always be

Enjoy it mike FLYING FREE !!!!!

VICTIM OF PTSD

As a veteran like those before
Many of us have seen war
Injuries invisible to the naked eye
In our mind we ask ourselves why

With all the bad that we have seen
We hope this is just a bad dream
Our memories won't disappear
In itself this gives us fear

When we were away we had each other
Watching out like sister and brother
But now we are home safe at last
Hopefully try to forget the past

Then night time falls
And our minds do wonder
Did i make a fatal blunder
No no not I it is the thunder

The bangs that go of in his head
Make him hide in his bed
He can not sleep it won't disappear
Yes I'm sure he'll shed a tear

Back in that place he once had been
Reliving the events he had seen
The smell the noise back in the mind
Shouting screaming feeling blind

Feeling lost and on his own
Fear, anxiety, depression have grown
But being proud and no cry for help
Man up son you have your health

But the mind will overcome
Unless something can be done
He does need help a listening ear
So he can process all that he does fear

He is human his mind is active
For his country his life he'd give
But alas many didn't make it back
Back home to raise the Union Jack

So to absent friend's I raise a glass
I'm sure this battle is not the last
Until we meet at the pearly gates
Spread the word about lost mates

REMEMBER THOSE FALLEN

Alas it is that time of year
When we all shed a tear
For absent soldiers who went before
In faraway lands fighting a war

From Ypres to the Somme
And further afield
Too many men
Far too young to be killed

Then more recent events did occur
In places some think mighty obscure
Places such as Iraq
Some families wishing daddy was back

Other places such as Afghanistan
Fighting for freedom of the condemned man
Not knowing who the enemy was
And being taken for this cause

Reminiscent of troubles near by
In places such as NI
I know this may upset a few
But all these conflicts are very true

I know I have missed quite a few
Such as the Falklands War and Bosnia too
Many countries where we have served
For human rights to be observed

They defended our country
With all there might
Never giving up the fight
Even in the dark of night

Remembering the fallen
Is not a one day event
They left too early
This was not meant

They are remembered daily by
Us that are left
There legacy will always live on
If we all remember what job they done

R.I.P my brothers in Arms
Until together we serve in heavens farm
Looking after one and all
Dancing with angels at the ball

REJECTION

Fear of rejection can come to us all
Feeling alone like facing the wall
All the outside just staring in
If only they could see what is within

Not feeling the spirit from all around
Just want to hide, open up the ground!
Rejection can come in many forms
From playground antics and college dorms

It can even turn up in a relationship
Too change this one shoot from the hip
To tackle rejection do it head on
Find out why and remain strong

Is it emotional or is it social
Both of these are psychological
They can be treated and sorted out
But remain calm try not to shout

Rejection can cause anger and aggression
External and even inward explosion
Don't blame yourself as this you don't need
Find a safe place, breathe slowly or read

A reason for this thought you won't find
It's a receptor buried deep in the mind
Studies say it's from out evolutionary past
They managed, so keep calm have a blast

Emotional pain is hard to ignore
Stay positive and don't become a bore
Pick yourself up and find the light
Then your life will start to be bright
Keep working on the little things
Then you will find what happiness brings

REMEMBER THOSE FALLEN

Alas it is that time of year
When we all shed a tear
For absent soldiers who went before
In faraway lands fighting a war

From Ypres to the Somme
And further a field
Too many men
Far too young to be killed

Then more recent events did occur
In places some think mighty obscure
Places such as Iraq
Some families wishing daddy was back

Other places such as Afghanistan
Fighting for freedom of the condemned man
Not knowing who the enemy was
And being taken for this cause

Reminiscent of troubles near by
In places such as NI
I know this may upset a few
But all these conflicts are very true

I know I have missed quite a few
Such as the Falklands War and Bosnia too
Many countries where we have served
For human rights to be observed

They defended our country
With all there might
Never giving up the fight
Even in the dark of night

Remembering the fallen
Is not a one day event
They left too early
This was not meant

They are remembered daily by
Us that are left
There legacy will always live on
If we all remember what job they done

R.I.P my brothers in Arms
Until together we serve in heavens farm
Looking after one and all
Dancing with angels at the ball

Printed in Great Britain
by Amazon